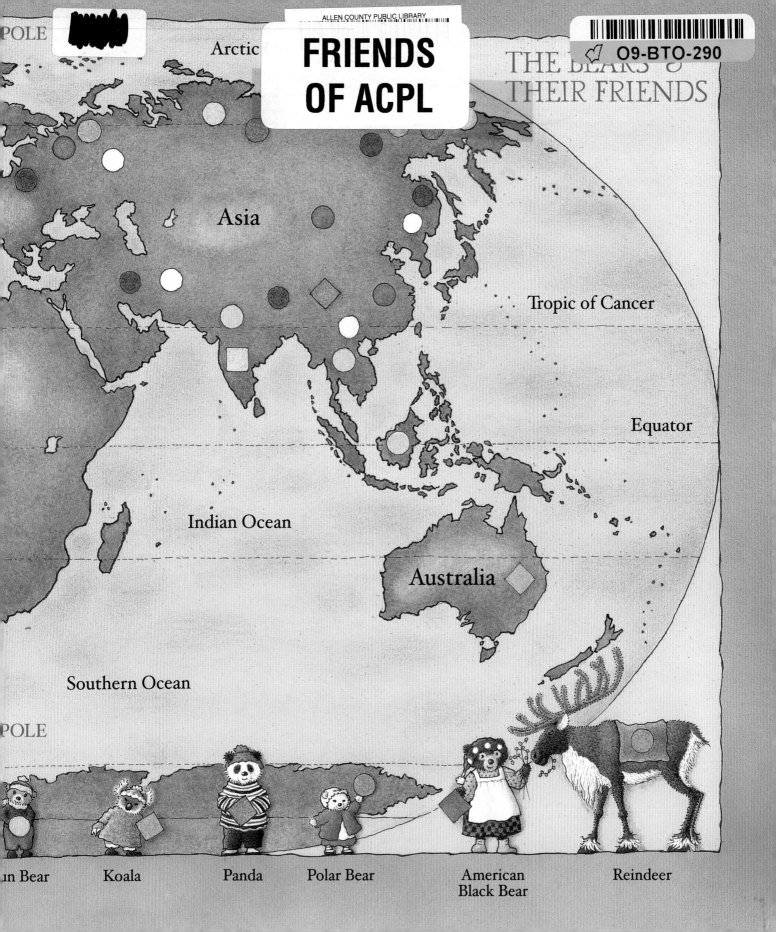

POLE

Arctic

THE BEARS &
THEIR FRIENDS

Asia

Tropic of Cancer

Equator

Indian Ocean

Australia

Southern Ocean

POLE

n Bear   Koala   Panda   Polar Bear   American   Reindeer
                                                                    Black Bear

THE CHRISTMAS BEARS

CHRIS CONOVER

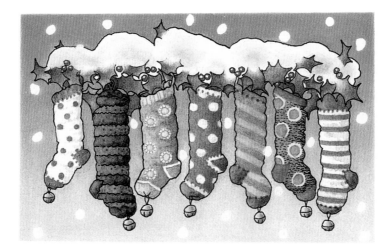

Farrar Straus Giroux

New York

For Edwin Doremus, with loving thanks

Distributed in Canada by Douglas & McIntyre Ltd.
Color separations by Chroma Graphics PTE Ltd.
Printed and bound in the United States of America by Phoenix Color Corporation
Designed by Jonathan Bartlett
First edition, 2008
1 3 5 7 9 10 8 6 4 2

www.fsgkidsbooks.com

Library of Congress Cataloging-in-Publication Data
Conover, Chris.
    The Christmas bears / Chris Conover.— 1st ed.
        p. cm.
    Summary: Santa Bear's seven cubs watch as their father loads the sleigh with toys to
deliver on Christmas Eve.
    ISBN-13: 978-0-374-33275-4
    ISBN-10: 0-374-33275-4
    [1. Christmas—Fiction. 2. Santa Claus—Fiction. 3. Bears—Fiction. 4. Stories in rhyme.]
I. Title.

PZ8.3.C7657Ch 2008
[E]—dc22
                                                                                        2007029295

CHRISTMAS IS COMING!

Our little house has a wreath on the door,
Cookies are baking, good things are in store.

We seven cubs print cards by the dozens,
And mail them to all our friends and cousins.

Down at Pa's workshop we make merry noise,
And he invites us to try out the toys.

Our Christmas Eve supper includes every treat
That bears and their friends enjoy most to eat.

With toys to deliver, Pa jumps in his sleigh.
Soon he and his team are off and away.

We dress our tree in green, gold, and red,
Give Mama kisses and climb into bed.

We're snug in our quilts till the sun peeps out,
Then we jump up with a whoop and a shout—

MERRY CHRISTMAS!

Arctic Circle

Europe

North America

Atlantic Ocean

Afric

Pacific Ocean

South America

Tropic of Capricorn

Antarctic Circle

Brown Bear   Spectacled   Snowy Owl   Cardinal   Moon Bear   Sloth Bea
              Bear